D0571613

E RAU
Rau, Dana Meachen
Shoo, crow! Shoo!

082506

SEP 1 5 2006

ROCKFORD PUBLIC LIBRARY
Rockford, Illinois
www.rockfordpubliclibrary.org
815-965-9511

Shoo, Crow! Shoo!

Written by Dana Meachen Rau
Illustrated by Mary Galan Rojas

Reading Advisers:

Gail Saunders-Smith, Ph.D., Reading Specialist

Dr. Linda D. Labbo, Department of Reading Education,
College of Education, The University of Georgia

LEVEL A

A COMPASS POINT
EARLY READER

ROCKFORD PUBLIC LIBRARY

For Nicole

A Note to Parents

As you share this book with your child, you are showing your new reader what reading looks like and sounds like. You can read to your child anywhere—in a special area in your home, at the library, on the bus, or in the car. Your child will associate reading with the pleasure of being with you.

This book will introduce your young reader to many of the basic concepts, skills, and vocabulary necessary for successful reading. Talk through the details in each picture before you read. Then read the book to your child. As you read, point to each word, stopping to talk about what the words mean and the pictures show. Your child will begin to link the sounds of the letters with the look of the words that you and he or she read.

After your child is familiar with the story, let him or her read the story alone. Be careful to let the young reader make mistakes and correct them on his or her own. Be sure to praise the young reader's abilities. And, above all, have fun.

Gail Saunders-Smith, Ph.D.
Reading Specialist

Compass Point Books
3109 West 50th Street, #115
Minneapolis, MN 55410

Visit Compass Point Books on the Internet at *www.compasspointbooks.com* or e-mail your request to *custserv@compasspointbooks.com*

Library of Congress Cataloging-in-Publication Data

Rau, Dana Meachen, 1971–
  Shoo, Crow! Shoo! / by Dana Meachen Rau ; illustrated by Mary Rojas.
      p. cm. — (Compass point early reader)
  Summary: A scarecrow is too friendly to do the job for which it was made.
  ISBN 0-7565-0072-9
      [1. Scarecrows—Fiction. 2. Stories in rhyme.] I. Rojas, Mary. II. Title. III. Series.
  PZ8.3.R232 Sh 2001
  [E]—dc21
                                                                    00-011844

© 2001 by Compass Point Books
All rights reserved. No part of this book may be reproduced without written permission from the publisher. The publisher takes no responsibility for the use of any of the materials or methods described in this book, nor for the products thereof.
Printed in the United States of America.

Old shirt.

Old pants.

Stuff them both
with hay.

Pumpkin head.

Draw a face.

Scare
those crows away!

pumpkin
patch

13

Hang him up.

Hang him high.

We have to tie
his shoe.

Now our scarecrow
is all done.

Go now!
Shoo, crow! Shoo!

23

Word List

(In this book: 36 words)

a	hay	scarecrow
all	head	shirt
away	high	shoe
both	him	shoo
crow	his	stuff
crows	is	them
done	now	those
draw	old	tie
face	our	to
go	pants	up
hang	pumpkin	we
have	scare	with

About the Author
Dana Meachen Rau's favorite time of year is the fall. She loves watching the leaves turn colors, feeling the chilly air, and raking leaves into piles. When she was little, she used to make scarecrows out of old flannel shirts and jeans and set them in the yard. Today, Dana lives in Farmington, Connecticut, with her husband, Chris, and son, Charlie, and writes lots of children's books.

About the Illustrator
Mary Galan Rojas works full-time as a freelance illustrator. She enjoys working on children's materials. The illustrations in this book were created on a Macintosh computer using several software programs. Mary lives in San Antonio, Texas, with her husband, Chris, their son, Matthew, and their nephew, Michael.